Craig D. Smith

Midnight Pieces

Twenty Poems

&

One Short Story

Craig D. Smith

Copyright © 2019 by Craig D. Smith

Requests for permission to make copies of
any part of the work should be emailed to:
Craig D. Smith
CDS.Literary@gmail.com
Or
c/o One-Eighty Films, Inc.
4242 SE Milwaukie
Portland, Oregon 97202
info@oneeightyfilms.com

Graphics Design: Craig D. Smith
Author Photo: Laura J. Tenny
First publication: December 2019

Library of Congress Cataloging-in-publication Data
Smith, Craig D. (Craig Donald), 1949 –

Midnight Pieces / Craig D. Smith
Published, 2019
ISBN: 978-0-578-60894-5
Printed in the United States of America

DEDICATION

For those who encourage...
For those who edify...
For those who inspire...
And for those who know midnights...

And for Laura,
Jenny & Abby

Craig D. Smith
Portland, OR
2019

TABLE OF CONTENTS

Craig D. Smith

THE OUTLOOK (A FORWARD)

I believe I began writing poetry when my teacher, Mrs. Adler, encouraged her High School English Literature class to seek "inspiration" to write an assigned poem. That meant my friend Dennis and I, enthusiastically took her advice and drove his jeep the next Saturday on a precarious route up to a remote forest-fire-lookout station. There one could scan the hills and valleys of Oregon's coast range and hopefully seek a level of enlightenment that would produce a good grade. I am not sure what Dennis wrote and I don't recall my own, but it did produce a certain exciting and dangerous perspective on poetry.

And so with that danger - exposed - poetry came to find me! It gradually placed empty notebooks before me. Slowly, over time, it drove an addiction to fill them with bits and pieces of emotion, imagination, ideas and fantasy. Its instruction was not heeded for the praise of others, but was for my own heart. Its apprenticeship trained feeling's expression, which in life, is sometimes desperately needed. I have found that personally true, and sorely so, but also wonderfully, clarifyingly and cathartically so.

Here offered are twenty poems from over the years, birthed after midnight in many cases; three of which were written by my late wife who turned words better than I. She inhabits the color of many of the others here presented...

... and there is one short story, which carries some of what imagination and poetry has taught. All are for your appreciation, your feelings and consideration... and that is why I have put them together herein. I hope you will enjoy.

Finally, thank you Mrs. Adler, and thank you Dennis. You and I survived that journey and poetry followed us home.

Craig D. Smith

MIDNIGHT PIECES

PARIS

We picked the wrong Paris.
Too late in the season,
Too early to be real.
I remember you speaking,
(Over candles and wine)
Of the old cathedral down the way;
How its shadows would
Always empty you.
We were both lost then...
You in your shadows,
I lighting candles;
And somewhere in between
Stood Paris.

November 1968

JAVA

We met over coffee spoons,
Measuring out our lives.
Pretending from empty cups...

The spring rain
On the roof,
Against the window,
On the umbrellas as they passed.

Was washing the day
Into the evening,
Down the wet streets
And into the gutters of the tungsten lit park...

And we walked.
It was not quite
As cold.
And our hands were warm...

March 1969

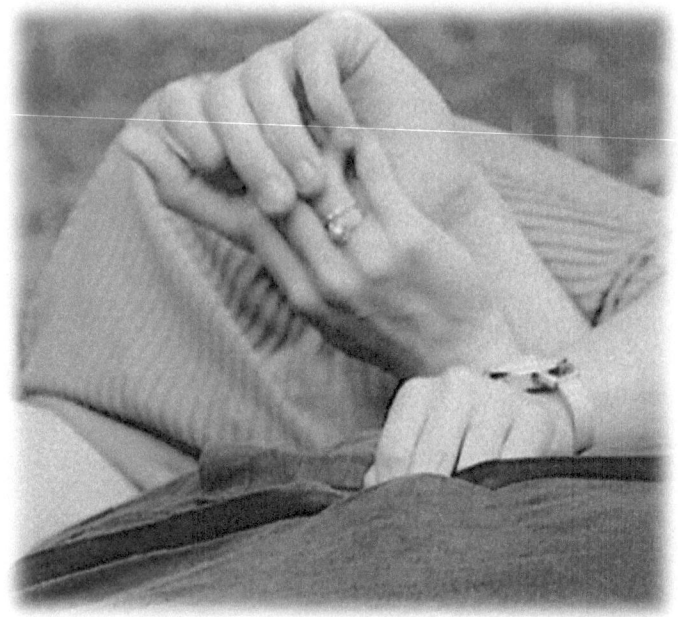

Temps d'amour

Oh, feel this loving time,
That wakes us from our sleep,
To dark and silent music,
That beckons soft and sweet,
And transforms this lonely darkness,
With our hearts now intertwined -
So, come near, let me whisper,
As we feel this loving time.

Oh, feel this loving time,
As it breaks upon our lives,
And shines a sparkling starlight,
In the heavens of your eyes.
It speaks in fragile kisses,
Of the precious warmth we find
As you're near to me in whispers,
And we feel this loving time.

Oh, feel this loving time,
That wraps us in its grace,
To hold us in a presence,
And offer true embrace.
The wonder of these hours,
No hand can truly scribe -
So, come near. Let me whisper,
As we feel this loving time.

July 1980

LASTING JOYS

Three poems by Candy Smith

"Of the journey of life she wrote thus far,
small moments of thoughts, simply for their own sake."

Watercolor by L.P. Ponor

ANNIVERSARY

The first colors gently stained the matte with care.
They were soft, without form... not quite there.
The tints of spring and honeyed summer
Traveled in harmony, content, beside each other.

Then the brush whispered over the vibrant hues,
Beginning to join the shades, now one from two.
Shyly blending at their first touch;
The colors melded into gold and amethyst.

Form gathered itself within the canvas borders,
Blooms from the field, grasses and flowers,
Curling leaves and twisting vines of green,
Veiled themselves in gauze; a watercolor dream.

Those first careful shades which gently stained,
Show themselves now a pastel rainbow intertwined.
The flowers which peek from behind the leaves,
Hint of the warming sun, of shells, and the blue of seas.

The brush glides on to show yet more petals and blades,
It continues to mix and swirl its lively shades.
And so, on it goes; the blending of one from two...
The shading, the silhouetting... of me and you.

Candy Smith
February 1, 1979

Lantern of Time

Pale...
Not so pale as the moon,
Only reserved in expressing
Joy.

Joy...
At greeting the night;
The charcoal friend of
Many good times.

Times...
The moments that sigh,
For escape from within
The Lantern.

Lantern...
A candle of light and secrets
That leads us, true
To all.

All...
In the pale, joyous lantern of time
We souls rest
One and all.

Candy Smith
July 1967

WHAT COLOR BE HIS EYES?

What color be his eyes?
They twinkle with wryness and life.
It is hard, sir, to hold their gaze,
In that they see through my heart's soul -
But, you asked the color –
Blue – yes, they are blue.

And what of his hair?
Many times, it bends, here and there,
Tucking in around about his head.
With softest touch and certain finish.
But, you asked the color –
Muted brown – yes, his hair is brown.

And what of his smile?
His smile is soft, meant to beguile.
Yet humble is its truth and warmth,
Which holds you sure and even, sir.
But, you asked of his smile –
Kind – yes, his smile is kind.

What say you of his soul?
It is gentle, friend; soft it grows
With mercy felt of heaven;
Known of faults and feeling.
But you asked of his soul –
Careful – yes, his soul is careful.

And is he yours?
He is not - yet, my dear love.
But to this end, I endure.
For that time comes soon, and soon will be.
Is he mine? Surely, and the joy of my life...
If but he ask of me.

Candy Smith
March 1967

LAMENTATIONS

LAMENT

You have been just a memory
for such a long time now.
Something I touch - when I touch
those things we shared.
No longer a bright light
that spots my vision,
Or a fussing dream that migrates
into some raw nerve.
But you wake me from the earth
as the seams of these days,
Weaken, soften and separate.
one by one the outer fabrics
...fall away;

And I notice, every once and a while
I find myself naked.
Making bumbling account
of how I have fooled myself...

...that you don't still inhabit
              every breath I take.

December 2003

SNAPSHOTS

There was a different life;
In that small time,
In that love of mine,
That seemed to be forever,
Where captured moments
Display themselves like
Demons;
Dark and haunting.
Now in softer emptiness;
Waiting for another life.

There was a different time;
In that small place;
In that love of yours;
Beneath red leaves
And April rains;
And summers like
Flashbulbs,
Momentary and bright;
Latent in my memory's eyes;
Holding life in another way.

There was a different place;
In that heartbeat;
In that momentary light,
In this yearning touch,
In that grievous scene.
Pictures wailing in
Whispers;
Colored songs and lullabies
Stilled, in a silent
Shuttered eye.

October 1996

MISS YOU MORE

Sometimes I miss you more,
So, I dance with your ghost
In the dark;
In morning's early hours,
Your head on my shoulder;
A phantom delight,
of some secret time,
Where now we cannot touch.

Sometimes I miss you more,
As some sad film flickers
Into tragedy;
My heart is pulled
Toward unconnected feelings,
Seeing finally
What few things
I have held back of you.

Sometime I miss you more,
When I discover that I am
Cut deeply
With the shards of our life;
Those things left to tempt me
To resurrect you.
For you still intoxicate me.
I bleed, and miss you more.

November 2016

QUIET TIME

Was it in my springtime youth,
Or winter's yesterday?
Your face and eyes smiled at me
Across the tablecloth.
The things we said in the mornings.
The things we said at night;
If once I could recall again
Would soothe my thirst like ice...
on hot afternoons.

Was it in my springtime youth,
Or winter's yesterday?
The kiss I felt to wake my days
Was full of autumn skies.
The lyric of your laughter,
The dancing of your love;
If memory's life could rise again
It would lift this heart like song...
on gray days.

Those days were for you and me,
That was our time.
This time is now quietness,
Brushed with waiting...
Till sleeps slips close beside me,
To kiss my eyes and dreams;
And paints you there, in quiet time;
Till dawn that canvas cleans.

July 1994

WINTER COAT

Morning, as always seems like
A hand, tapping on the shoulder.
Cold - I join the advance; silent,
And I wear my winter coat.

There were kinder articles of life,
At times, the passionate wear
Of more durable days.
Clothing for simpler ways...

But, I wear a winter coat
For times like these.
For the sun, seems under battle.
Light and warmth wrinkled with wear.

And we wage a war of retreat...
Until coldness stops our feet, frost seizes us,
And finally erases our name from some great book.
Tragedy reminds us with outstretched hand.

I would forsake this coat
But for that touch! If I could...
But within the summer textures of life;
My thoughts of late while strolling the shore.

Wind and dreams, breaking, rolling onto sand,
The softness of a kiss.
The music of laughter,
As children ride the melodies of that muse...

I see today's wind is gentle...
The waves roll back,
And this winter coat blows loose.

July 1997

TAPS

TAPS

The triangle
had stars,
handed between hands
between lives, traded,
folded like endings.

Unlike other
moving cloth of life.
pure white - honor
now tucked in heaven's folds,
dreams put away.

And crimson stripes;
sacrifice offered;
handed between hands,
traded for stars,
folded like endings.

September 1996

THE WALL IN D.C.

Your faces haunt my thoughts and dreams,
Your faces pass before me,
Like pictures from some time machine,
From gray stone, each imploring.
From silent lips,
Now whispers slip,
Oh, hear the quiet roaring!
By granite wall, we soon recall,
The troubles of our warring.

Your names I read, across my face,
Beside me friends are crying,
Like family in a dying place,
Like enemies of lightning.
We touch your shapes,
That now create,
One fierce word skyward soaring,
Of what we loose, if once we choose,
The troubles of our warring.

March 1995

SOLDIER'S LULLABY

Hear no more,
The song of war,
And do not heed the drum.
Fear no more,
The cannon roar,
Nor heat of battles done.

But lay you now,
In meadow down,
Midst comrades you have loved.
There find you sleep,
With deep retreat,
And no more thought of guns.

December 1995

REFLECTIONS

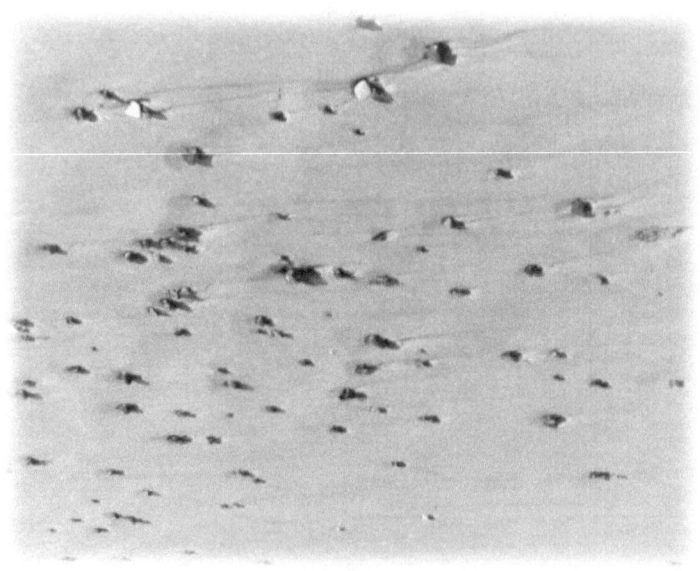

SUMMER SONG

I will let the Summer hunt me
This year along some beach,
Wasting the sand,
Until I am caught in Summer's claws,
Unfeeling, like some small gray quarry;
Unmercifully torn from normal life...

Oh! To stand before the great sea,
Or the titans of the mountains,
Washed and raw, as hot and cleansing
Elements burn my eyes clean...

I will follow Summer's river
Down her canyon alleys where,
Trapped before some giant rock,
Her waters will press life into me,
Embrace and feel all that is my soul...
Until she crushes me with a gentle finger,
And lifts me, reborn...

And could I not, while impaled on some
Midnight dream, hear the summer night
Whisper in my ear, and beckon with diamonds,
And jewels, and intoxicating fragrance.
I must go with her. I must seize her...
Before the lion of summer slips from view,
And Orion chases her across the sky.

I feel the warm breath of the Zephyr's wind
Breathing into my throat
The kiss of fire, and lie of eternity.
Standing like a child,
My hand extended,
bucket in hand,
I am led into a new slavery...

The summer moon has three lives
I will take them all...
Take them all!
To pack them like a miser
Into some small hole before a hearth.

Later, closing the cold blinds
I will bring them out...
And burn their mysteries
Like hot coals,
Into my pale skin.

March 1996

THE RETURN

How could I be serious?
I wait for the bus that carries your smile.
I wait like a monk in a monastery,
Bent in silent prayer.

From packs of Camels
Tobacco incense ascends,
Then falls again,
Like my emotions.

This place I live
Runs like a river through my life.
Flooding and swelling –
Tearing down bare trees,
Dragging them through me.

Then you leave again,
And the dry season comes;
The empty shore.
And I wait for the bus that carries your smile.

Yet I regret every minute ticking past
To join the waters of fear.
How could I be serious?

Larger and wider the river grows...
While I wait for your smile.

February 1999

KIND PEOPLE

Different tones sound and ring through life.
Enigmas each, mysterious or fair.
Seen patterned like glass, colored;
Finally known....
"Oh, kind people", I whisper, "kind people."

Changing smiles in minutes, each to meet each face.
Words real and quiet, they wing, they softly calm.
Like fragrant air;
Fashioning renewal...
"Oh, kind people", I whisper, "kind people."

Arms together, weak soft touch of fingers now,
Find ragged tears, poor life's wear.
Mended cloth then stayed by compassion's thread;
Darkness lit... and rescue seen,
"Oh, kind people", I whisper, "kind people."

Kissed by blue, strolling clouds witness past.
Silver rays, beneath such eyes.
A word, a spirit on lips' unspoken joy -
Why so life? Why life is so?
"Oh, kind people", I whisper, "kind people."

October 1996

VILLA

It rests - like silence,
in framed open window,
with closed doors and whispers,
and poplars like rhythms,
like rhythms in azure,
through hushed shadowed villa.
with shining halls empty...
and vines; parallel vineyards,
in languishing quiet,
with rolling sun pressing,
and Spanish strings flowing,
along curtains and breezes,
and touching now curving, like soft skin
and falling, like fall away shadows...
and passing of candles,
and passing of candles,
like passing of candles... to night.

They lay - fragrant courtyards,
of strange haunting twilight,
with flowers and music,
and hills like embraces,
like embraces now hinting,
midst trellis and winding,
through lingering gardens...
and gates opened thresholds,
with passionate stillness,
and hidden blooms waiting,
in delicate fingers,
by tiles and fences,
where closeness is hoping,
like hope's waking fabric...
and fragile night's dreaming,
and fragile night's dreaming,
like fragile night's dreaming... to dawn.

February 1999

43

Sweet Lady of the Moon

(Within the fairy ring)

She spins, the fickle flickering sprite,
In whitish, flaxen fairy light,
Seeking play and hid from sight,
Reaching hands out to the night,
Singing dreams and taking flight,
Sweet lady of the moon.

Her rings of flowers circling goes,
Near us still, still water flows,
Quicker each, the ring enclose,
'Round mists where mystic music rose,
And beneath our feet their song imposed,
Sweet lady of the moon.

Now wraps her bluish fragrance fair,
As shining wings, wing through that aire.
Winding, flashing, sparkling hair,
I'm wishing, wishes with you there,
In that wondrous other-where,
Sweet lady of the moon.

Craig Smith
5/17/1996

Craig D. Smith

EMMA

(I rest as one already dead, except for time)

After that day, you were in black;
I had my umbrella, and carried a hat...
You straightened my tie
With nothing to say...
As church bells were tolling
A curious way.

Oh Emma please answer, just how are you?
What secrets do you keep?
What fates have you sealed?
Whose hearts have you taken?
Yes, taken away, with a smile on your lips,
But your rapture delayed?
But still, I must ask,
As your work, I now trace.
Yes, who lies there Emma
At night in my place.

Some persons unknown,
Say I want you to die.
Some challenge my honor,
Some tell you that lie.
But Emma you've shown them!
It's no amateur play...
The hand you have chosen,
The power you obey.
You've sacrificed love,
Oh Emma, I know!
We both have experienced that particular foe.
The empty wine glass
That now hides your disguise,
Can't conceal the lingering rage in your eyes.

So Emma please tell me, just how are you?
These secrets in our hearts...
Have we both played the fool?
Our lives we have given, and seen thrown away.
As the proof of our trust
In their hands, then betrayed.
But still, I musk ask,
As my life, I now face.
Yes, who lies there Emma
At night in my place?

After that day... I dressed in black.
Under my umbrella, I wore a hat...
With a pin in my tie,
Like a bug on display.
The fog was descending...
Like petals in May.

September 1995

ONE SHORT STORY

PICTURES OF EMILY

I believe there are scenes; pictures from our lives, that become tempered memories hardened into the mind; images that are perhaps the last things to go, each, former pieces of our days we guard until some final confusion melts our recollections into elemental things.

I have such pictures.

There is one! A young woman laboring in silence over a growing sculpture of a horse. She is alone in the rear of the classroom, but not really. She is unaware there are interested eyes that watch each movement. Her hands and fingers are pressing and twisting pieces of clay into different shapes that are remarkably transforming into muscles and sinew of the great animal she is sculpting. There is an instructor also, in the front of the room. I do hear his words explaining clay; its substance, its makeup; the tools; their use. Words unconnected to reality until they collide and are totally explained as I glance over to see the actuality of the equine creation of clay in progress, and its tactile muse.

Later, my fingers roll that same material in my hand. It is not the words of instruction, which make it move in my palm, but rather the example of this young woman's ease as she touches her handiwork.

I look again... another picture. The horse now is set aside but I see it is awake; it is awake in fury. Its mane flares in waves of fire behind the curve of a half-finished Arabian neck. It looks annoyed, frustrated with its own incompleteness. The legs are still only wire stalks hinting of life, anxious to run. I slow my own work of softening clay and there is a rising mercy in me to press it somewhere on that animal, however awkwardly, to give it fullness. Then I realize the creator; she is behind me, then beside me. She is here in this class to help... to aid the instruction.

I turn back to my own primitive inanimate beast, embarrassed. It is something like Porky... I think. It is the shape of that small and humorous pig. Her hands reach out to touch the flat nose and small ears. She suddenly laughs to herself as I watch her feel the shape of the little fellow. Then I look into her face, soft, bright, quiet and realize... she is blind.

I am feeling... opened... self-conscious with a certain awe. That feeling when someone famous and powerful stands next to you and you have no words. The thought comes and passes quickly, "Would I trade such

*misfortune for a sight that lifted earth to life?"
I remember the clay in my palm and that same
mercy which I felt for the horse began to gain
a different focus.*

*Now, I recall a picture of her hands covering
my cartoon of clay... an inept shape that we
then begin to change in concert.*

*Will I remember the words, all the words of
that late summer class? I will remember her
picture, and the horse over those weeks,
growing steadily. First, to stumble, then
stand, trot... finally gallop over fields like a
wild steady storm.*

*And the animal was possessed! I watched as
her touch bent it here and there. Its nostrils
flared. She reined it, turned it. She urged it
through imagined meadows, dashing through
valleys and down steep mountains, throwing
up dust and rock and dirt, plunging headlong
down to where I would follow her as she
walked and cooled the foaming, steaming
figure she loved.*

*And I extended pictures of my world as I led
them cautiously into that summer, and
summer's end, into a frame even more bold
when the embers of fall began to burn and
descend upon us; that leaf colored rain.*

And the wind blew the cooling sunshine of the season into our faces. I talked and she listened to my descriptions of the invisible thing called light that transfigured all things. A picture for her. Color... angles... motion... the space and medium of my elaborate visual world portrayed within the grand and formal events of autumn, but thrown against an unsuitable canvas.

But, weeks later we walked in a quieter way, bundled in warm coats and jackets, breathing out visible frosty breath along the riverfront where the park wound close to the water. There the water flowed like liquid blue desire towards the heart of the sea, transporting reflected puffs of clouds. Clouds that would, in not too many more days, become oppressive with rain; dark, with a broody chill.

Yet, my descriptions were only odd pictures to her, strange and awkwardly finger-painted with a palate of meaningless vowels and consonants. When I looked at her she had turned away. I watched as she took several steps and finding a bench, sat down. Her eyes were moist.

"Will you, sit here?" She asked tentatively.

I knew by then why she looked so alone and I took that portrait in, a jealous thing to see her there, solitary. It was a selfish satisfaction. I sat down next to her. She tilted her head slightly and leaned against my shoulder. I knew before she spoke. "It... is done. Finished." She said with a quiet voice. "It is... away. Nothing."

"Oh!" I replied.

I had watched as she finished the animal. I awaited each concluding motion... every contact... slower, and more hesitant... until she finally ran her hands wholly in benediction over the living thing... then stopped and stood and did not reach for it again. She had set it free.

We sat for several minutes without speaking. My eyes finally closed and I retreated to that gray behind my mind, passing the illumination of dark light, and into a gallery where her sculpture had roamed. I found her there. She stood alone; she was a picture looking at me.

I noticed her shiver... then I felt her fingers touch my face.

July 2000

ILLUSTRATIONS

1. COVER: **Vintage Key, *Book and Pocket Watch. The Key is in Time*** - Jonas Verstuyft, Dreamstime ID 48560810 (Licenced CC0 1.0)

2. PARIS: ***Rain in Paris*** *(Modified)* - Nicolas Vigier, flickr.com/photos/85825630 Public Domain - No Copyright ©

3. JAVA: ***Young Couple Walking*** - David Martyn, BigStock Photo ID: 915919 (Copyright: Extended license)

4. TEMPS D'AMOUR: ***Untitled Photo*** - Clem Onojeghuo, (Universal CC0 1.0)

5. ANNIVERSARY: ***Details within the Details*** – Linda Ponor (Modified watercolor ponorist@gmail.com – by permission)

6. LANTERN OF TIME: ***Lighted Lanterns - People releasing lanterns into the sky to welcome the Chinese Lantern Festival in Pingshi, Taiwan*** – Wally Santana, Associated Press ©

7. WHAT COLOR BE HIS EYES: ***Young Girl Writing a Love Letter*** - Pietro Antonio Rotari, (c. 1755, oil on canvas Norton Simon Museum) ©

8. LAMENTATIONS: ***Angel Statue,*** Linda Thomas, Publicdomainpictures.net, (CC0 Public Domain)

9. SNAPSHOTS: *Photo: **Jenny a Snapshot*** – Craig Smith

10. QUIET TIME: ***Autumn leaves -*** Oxfordian Kissuth, Commons.wikimedia.org (Creative Commons Attribution-Share Alike 3.0 Unported license)

11. MISS YOU MORE: ***Original Graphic: Tunnel*** – Craig Smith

12. WINTER COAT: ***Original Graphic Graphic: Coat*** – Craig Smith

13. TAPS: ***On Behalf of a Grateful Nation*** – Courtesy ARLINGTON NATIONAL CEMETARY

14. THE WALL IN DC: ***A Marine at Vietnam Memorial on 4th July 2002***. – Meutia Chaerani - Indradi Soemardjan, (Licensed for reuse under Creative Commons Licence Attribution - ShareAlike, 2.0 Generic CC BY-SA 2.0)

15. SOLDIER'S LULLABY: ***Tomb of the Unknown Soldier*** – Mark Fischer (Creative Commons.wikapedia.org Creative Commons Attribution-Share Alike 3.0 Unported license)

16. SUMMER SONG: ***Photo: Sand and Agates*** – Craig Smith

17. THE RETURN: ***Original Graphic: The Return*** – Craig Smith

18. *KIND PEOPLE: **"50/50"**, Library of Congress, ID cph.3c31892 1922 Public Domain* Ⓢ

19. VILLA: **A Tuscany villa in the valley at sunrise (Modified),** Evgord, ID 84485487 © (Dreamstime.com License CC0 1.0)

20. SWEET LADY OF THE MOON: **Surreal light in dark forest,** Ilkin Guliyev - Dreamstime Photo ID84385694 Modified Image, (Dreamstime.com License CC0 1.0)

21. EMMA: **Fog at Westminster, London**, George Tsiagalakis, (Licensed for reuse under Creative Commons Licence Attribution - ShareAlike, 2.0 Generic CC BY-SA 2.0)

22. A PICTURE OF EMILY: **Closeup-man and woman holding each other`s hands**, Yurolaitsalbert, ID 121903616 Dreamstime.com ©
    |

Craig D. Smith

ABOUT THE AUTHOR

Craig D. Smith currently lives in Portland, Oregon.

Midnight Pieces is his first book of poetry.

His other works include:

Within the Fire of Evening, a collection of original Science Fiction stories and

Everyman's War, a book based upon his father's experiences in WWII. He also wrote the screenplay for the award-winning film by the same name.

Midnight Pieces

Everyman's War – The Book

"Taut, lean, direct, unadorned, stunningly readable, this story of courage and love quietly becomes the Human Story of Courage and Love. I finished the last pages, thanked the Coherent Mercy for putting me in this bruised and blessed world, and called my dad."

Brian Doyle, author of **Thirsty for the Joy: Australian & American Voices**

AVAILABLE ON AMAZON.COM

Everyman's War – The Film

One man's hope… One man's courage…
Everyman's War.

Everyman's War 'Winner G.I. Film Festival'

"If I could package the mission of the GI Film
Festival into one two-hour film, it would be
"EVERYMAN'S WAR"

~Brandon L. Millet ~

President G.I. Film Festival 2008!

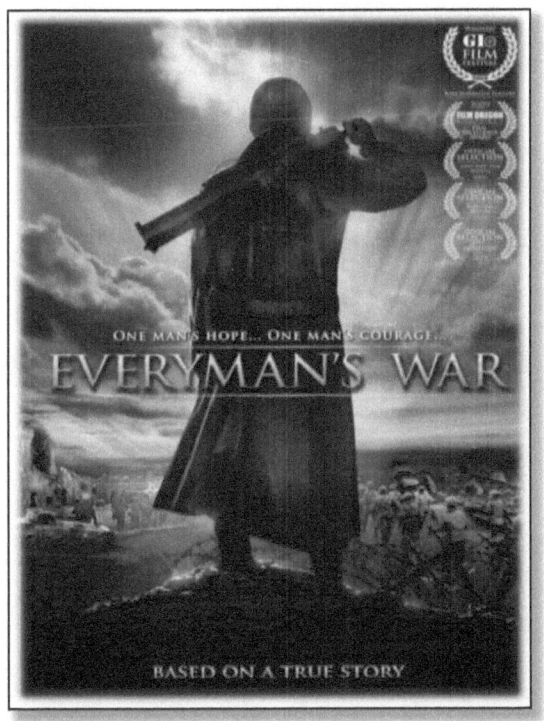

AVAILABLE ON AMAZON.COM

Within the Fire of Evening

"Within the Fire of Evening is science-fiction with a heart. It holds the glow of a warm, comforting, eerily familiar future. You will be taken to the stars where human civilization stubbornly refuses to die. You will be taken through time to a future Earth devastated by war. And woven through it all is a haunting yet uplifting nostalgia for days long past. The settings vary, the humanity doesn't. Here are nine tales that leave you with a yearning, "if only...""

John Olsen, author of *The Crystal Screen*

AVAILABLE ON AMAZON.COM